BUTTERFLIES

Written by Clara Reiff

HARCOURT BRACE & COMPANY

Orlando Atlanta Austin Boston San Francisco Chicago Dallas New York
Toronto London

Butterfly orange,

Butterfly blue,

Butterfly white,

Butterfly two.

Butterfly yellow,

Butterfly brown,

Fly butterfly, all around.